ABOUT THE BOOK

Eliza's daddy no longer lives with Eliza and her mommy, but across town with a new wife and children. Each Saturday when Eliza's daddy comes to take her to some special place, Eliza tries to gather her courage to ask him to take her to the really special place she longs to go—to his new home, to meet his new family—especially his stepdaughter, about her age, whom she imagines to be brighter and more beautiful than she.

IANTHE THOMAS

Eliza's Daddy

ILLUSTRATED BY MONETA BARNETT

HARCOURT BRACE JOVANOVICH

New York and London

Library of Congress Cataloging in Publication Data

Thomas, Ianthe, 1951-
Eliza's daddy.

(A Let me read book)
SUMMARY: Eliza wonders what her Daddy's daughter in his new marriage is like. She works up the courage to ask to visit his new home.
[1. Divorce—Fiction.   2. Fathers and daughters—Fiction]   I. Barnett, Moneta.   II. Title.
PZ7.T36693El   [Fic]   75-41343
ISBN 0-15-225400-5
ISBN 0-15-225401-3 pbk.

For Eric and Mandy

Eliza's daddy was a big, strong man
who didn't live with Eliza in her
house.

He lived down the block,
around the corner,
past Colucci's meat market,
way on the other side of town.
And he had a new family.

He didn't come to Eliza's house very
often, but when he did, he would sit on
the porch and say, "Tell your mother
we'll be back at five o'clock" or
"Tell your mother that you'll need
a sweater."

He would never tell Eliza's mother
anything, anytime, anywhere.
And he never called her "Honey"
anymore.
This made Eliza very sad.
She knew that her daddy and mommy
were divorced, though, and no matter
how much she wanted them
to live together again,
this just wasn't going to happen.

Now her daddy had a new family,
a new wife,
a new daughter,
and a new baby, who called
her father "Daddy."

Eliza's daddy lived with his new
family all week, but every
Saturday afternoon he would come
to Eliza's house to take her out.
"Where do you want to go today,
Eliza?" he would ask.
And Eliza would think very hard
of a special place to go
with her daddy.

Last week on their special day they went
to the zoo, and Eliza's daddy had let
her eat too much cotton candy.
He never said, "You've had enough junk,
Baby," the way he used to.

Instead, he let her eat five
cotton candy cones until she
was sticky and sick
all the way home.

Eliza had been dizzy.
Her mother had been angry.
And her father had said,
"I'm sorry, Eliza. I shouldn't have let
you eat so much."
Then he went over to the other side of
town where his new family lived.
That night, Eliza had a dream.

She dreamed she met her father's
new daughter.
Her father's new daughter's name was
Wonderful Angel Daughter.
Everyone in the world called her
Wonderful Angel Daughter.
Oh, she was beautiful!
Oh, she was smart!
She had been to a ranch in Arizona,
and she knew how to ride horses.

She came riding up to Eliza on a
beautiful black horse—the most
magnificent horse in the world.
His name was Wonderful Horse.
"Can you ride a horse, Eliza?"
asked Wonderful Angel Daughter.

"Yes," said Eliza softly,
even though she knew she couldn't.
"Well then, here's your horse."

Beautiful Wonderful Angel Daughter
laughed.
Out trotted the most flea-bitten donkey
Eliza had ever seen.

Eliza tried to get on the donkey, but he just sat down and started eating grass.

Eliza was begging him to get up when
she woke up.
"Oh, what a horrible dream," she thought
as she picked herself up from the floor.
She tried to go back to sleep,
but she couldn't.
All she could think about was her
father's new daughter.

"Just suppose she does have a horse,"
thought Eliza.
"Just suppose she has the most beautiful
black horse in the world.
Just suppose she's been to a ranch
in Arizona.
Maybe she has done everything in the
world," thought Eliza sadly.

Every day she thought more and more
about her daddy's new daughter.
Eliza wondered what kind of clothes
she wore.
She wondered if she could speak Spanish.
She wondered if she had a bicycle.
She wondered if she could stand on her
head without someone's holding her feet.
She wondered so much about her daddy's
new daughter that she decided to ask
him if she could come to his house.

On Friday night, Eliza set her clothes
out for Saturday.
She was going to wear her striped
overalls and her pointed-toe
cowboy boots.

Just before she got into bed, she stood
in front of the mirror practicing what
she was going to say to her daddy.
She decided to say,
"Daddy, may I come to your house?"
Eliza thought that this was the most
polite way to ask.

But on Saturday, when her father said,
"What do you want to do today, Eliza?"
she said,
"I want to . . . I want to . . . uh, I
want to . . . to go to the park."

"O.K.," said Daddy.
And they went to the park.

That night when she was
putting on her pajamas,
she said to herself,
"Next Saturday I'm really
going to ask him."
So she practiced saying,
"Daddy, may I come to your
house?" every single night
until she was sure she could
do it right.

On Saturday, before her father even had
a chance to ask her what she wanted to
do, Eliza said,

"Daddy, may I come to your house?"—just the way she had practiced all week.

"Do you really want
to go there, Eliza?"
her father asked.
"Yes, Daddy,"
she said.
"More than
anything else."

"O.K., Eliza," Daddy said.

They got in his car and drove all the
way across town—past Mrs. Wilkes,
sitting under her wisteria bush,

past a kitten crying in front of
Colucci's market—all the way over
to the other side of town.

All the way across town to a big house, where there was a girl about Eliza's age playing in the yard

and a baby, sitting in a yellow stroller,
who called Eliza's father "Daddy."

"Hi," said the girl, running up to Eliza.
"I'm Mandy."
"Hi. I'm Eliza."

"Can you ride a horse, Mandy?"
asked Eliza.
"No. I never have," said Mandy sadly.
"Neither can I," said Eliza.
"Why don't we ask Daddy to take us
riding today?" said Mandy, smiling.
"That would be great," said Eliza.

They ran to Eliza and Mandy's daddy
and asked him.

So he took them riding—together.

Ianthe Thomas was born in New York City and grew up in Hyde Park, New York. She attended Sarah Lawrence College for three years and then went to the Universidad de Coimbra to pursue her interest in sculpture. She has had one-woman shows of her wrought iron and mild steel pieces. Ms. Thomas, who has worked as a curriculum developer at the Education Development Center in Cambridge, Massachusetts, and as a teacher and researcher, is the author of four children's books. She and her husband, a film student and teacher, live in New York City.

Moneta Barnett was born and raised in Brooklyn, New York. She studied art at Cooper Union and the Brooklyn Museum Art School and has worked as a letterer, designer, and art director of a seriographic house. Ms. Barnett, a well-known illustrator of books for children, is also a painter and photographer. She lives in Brooklyn near Prospect Park, where she jogs every day with her Doberman pinscher.